Speaking in Green

Rolling into Peace

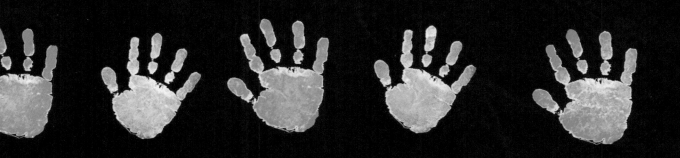

Written by: Erica D. Babino

Illustrated by: Robinson Pyles

Visit us on the Web

www.speakingingreen.org

Facebook: www.facebook.com/speakingingreen

lnstagram: speaking.in.green.series

ISBN: 978-0-9990271-0-3

For Alexandra, Delores, and Joseph

Angelique and Les

Resolutions Northwest

Manousso Mediation

and all who work to resolve conflict in the world.

TABLE OF CONTENTS

"Buenos Dias, mi amor," sang Gabriella's grandmother.

"Good morning, Abuela."

"Thank you for waking me," said Gabriella as she stretched towards the ceiling.

"Wake up, Petey Peace," said Gabriella.

"Morning time already?" asked Petey Peace wagging his tail.

"I'm still sleepy," he yawned.

"It's a great new day. Time to eat breakfast and walk to school," said Gabriella climbing out of bed.

"Let's have a wonderful day," Miss Emma said greeting each student at the door. "Please place your backpacks neatly in a cubby so that no one trips over them. Let's care for each other."

"OUCH! That hurt," yelled Jackson reaching for his foot underneath the wheel of Gabriella's backpack.

"Oh! Don't be a cry baby! My backpack isn't THAT heavy," said Gabriella as she rolled her bag away.

"What's wrong with you? Say you're sorry. I will never play with you again if you don't say it," muttered Jackson.

Gabriella paused then continued to walk away.

"Anyway, your backpack is ugly!" said Jackson pointing his finger towards Gabriella.

"Stop shouting at me. I didn't mean to do it. I don't know why all of you are so mean to me," said Gabriella tearfully.

During recess, Jalen, Cam, Alex, Zara, and Jackson gathered on the playground to talk.

"I'm tired of Gabriella's attitude. She will NOT hurt you again, Jackson," Alex said with a frown.

"I don't know why she acts that way," said Cam.

"Maybe she didn't mean to do it," said Zara.

"Do you think we could talk with her?" Jalen asked quietly.

Still feeling the pain in his foot, Jackson said, "I think we simply won't play with her anymore. Then she'll stop."

"I don't think that will change things," said Zara.

"Let's talk with Miss Emma," Jalen said walking towards the classroom. "She can help us. She'll know what to do."

"My goodness! What happened?" Miss Emma asked.

"I can see that everyone is upset."

"Gabriella smashed Jackson's foot with her backpack," Cam started.

"She refused to say she was sorry," Zara interjected.

"Really? What are your thoughts on finding a peaceful solution?" Miss Emma inquired.

"Maybe we could talk with each other," Alex suggested to the group.

"That sounds like a great idea. I know this can all be worked out by communicating. You're all sincere and compassionate children. We can always use our Green Words to make things better. It's important to feel joy instead of feeling sad and frustrated. Right?"

Everyone nodded in agreement.

"OK. Let's all stop and be quiet for just a minute before we speak," she said. "Take a deep breath and relax."

" OK. Let's listen attentively to one another. It's important to remain open and respect each other even if we don't agree with what someone else is saying. Everyone deserves a chance to tell their side of the story. We will pledge to P.A.W.S. in Yellow before we Speak in Green," said Miss Emma.

"Does everyone agree to a peaceful mediation?"

Ms. Emma
Live·Laugh·Teach

"Yes, Ma'am," said Cam twirling her hair.

"I do," Zara replied.

"That sounds good," Alex answered calmly.

"Cool," said Jalen with a big smile.

"Me too," murmured Jackson reluctantly.

"But ..." Gabriella paused. "Okay," she sighed.

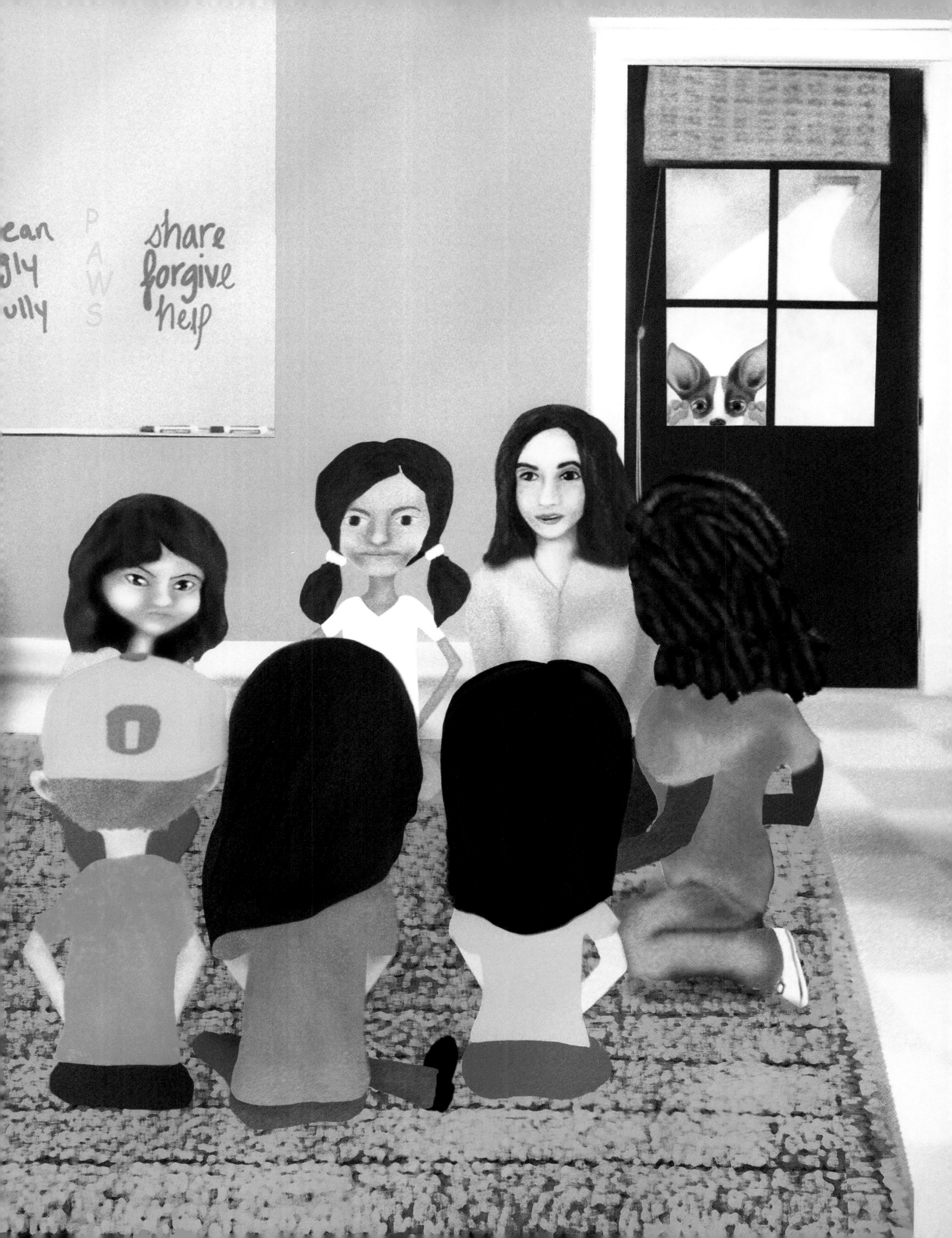

ean
gly
ully
P
A
W
S
share
forgive
help

"Jackson, please share your thoughts about what happened today," said Miss Emma encouragingly.

"Gabriella rolled over my foot ON PURPOSE!" Jackson said pointing his finger at Gabriella. "She KNEW I was sitting in my desk."

"Thank you for sharing that with us, Jackson," said Miss Emma.

"Now, Gabriella, what do you feel happened today?" Miss Emma asked turning to face her.

"I did roll my backpack over his foot, Miss Emma, but it was a MISTAKE! I didn't do it ON PURPOSE!"

"A mistake? Yeah. Right," said Jackson rolling his eyes. "That's why we decided not to play with you anymore."

"Shut up, Jackson!" shouted Gabriella. "You all never let me play with you anyway and you make fun of the way I talk. You don't like me. You only care about yourselves," cried Gabriella.

"We agreed to Speak in Green. Let's use a peaceful tone of voice, please," Miss Emma reminded the students. "Maybe I can speak with Gabriella and Jackson alone for a few minutes since it appears this happened between the two of them," Miss Emma said nearly whispering.

"I was listening to you, Gabriella and heard you say there was an accident this morning. Is that correct?" asked Miss Emma.

"Yes, Miss Emma. It REALLY was an accident," Gabriella responded.

"Maybe you and Jackson can talk together now." said Miss Emma.

"Please be respectful to one another and remember to use your Green Words."

"I would've said I was sorry, but you gave me such a nasty look," Gabriella said sadly. "I know I should've said it."

"Well, why didn't you?" Jackson asked.

"My feelings were hurt too!" cried Gabriella. "You yelled at me and everyone was staring. Since I moved here from Mexico, I feel like I'm invisible. I'm not. I'm right here. I know how to admit when I'm wrong.

"I'm sorry," she said wiping her tears.

"I didn't know you felt so badly, Gabriella. I had a choice too. I could've used my Green Words instead. Your backpack is cool. I really like the picture of Petey Peace on it,"

Jackson smiled extending his hand to help her stand.

"Maybe we should all talk now."

"We didn't realize we were hurting you, Gabriella. Thanks for sharing it with us. This won't happen with any other new student, "Alex said apologetically. "We can read and study spelling words together if you'd like."

"I'm sorry too," said Jackson.

"I understand, Gabriella. I was adopted from Vietnam. When I came to school, I didn't think the kids liked me either," said Cam. "They REALLY did! We like you too!"

"Some kids taunted me about my dreadlocks. I KNOW they're great!" said Jalen smiling and twisting his dreads.

"People say ugly things about my mother's hijab. I know it's because they don't understand," explained Zara. "It's great that we're all different! We must respect and love each other. I'm glad we're friends now, Gabriella."

"Thanks," said Gabriella wiping a tear from her eye. "I'm sorry too. I was frustrated and I took it out on Jackson."

"Sometimes we don't treat others well when we're hurting," said Petey Peace. "The best way to handle conflict is to do what?"

"SPEAK IN GREEN," everyone said smiling while giving each other high fives and fist bumps.

"NOW, can we all be friends?" inquired Jalen.

"That's great, Jalen! Let's make a pledge to be caring, understanding, and show empathy for each other. Does everyone agree?" asked Petey Peace.

"YES!" they all exclaimed. "Thank you, Petey Peace."

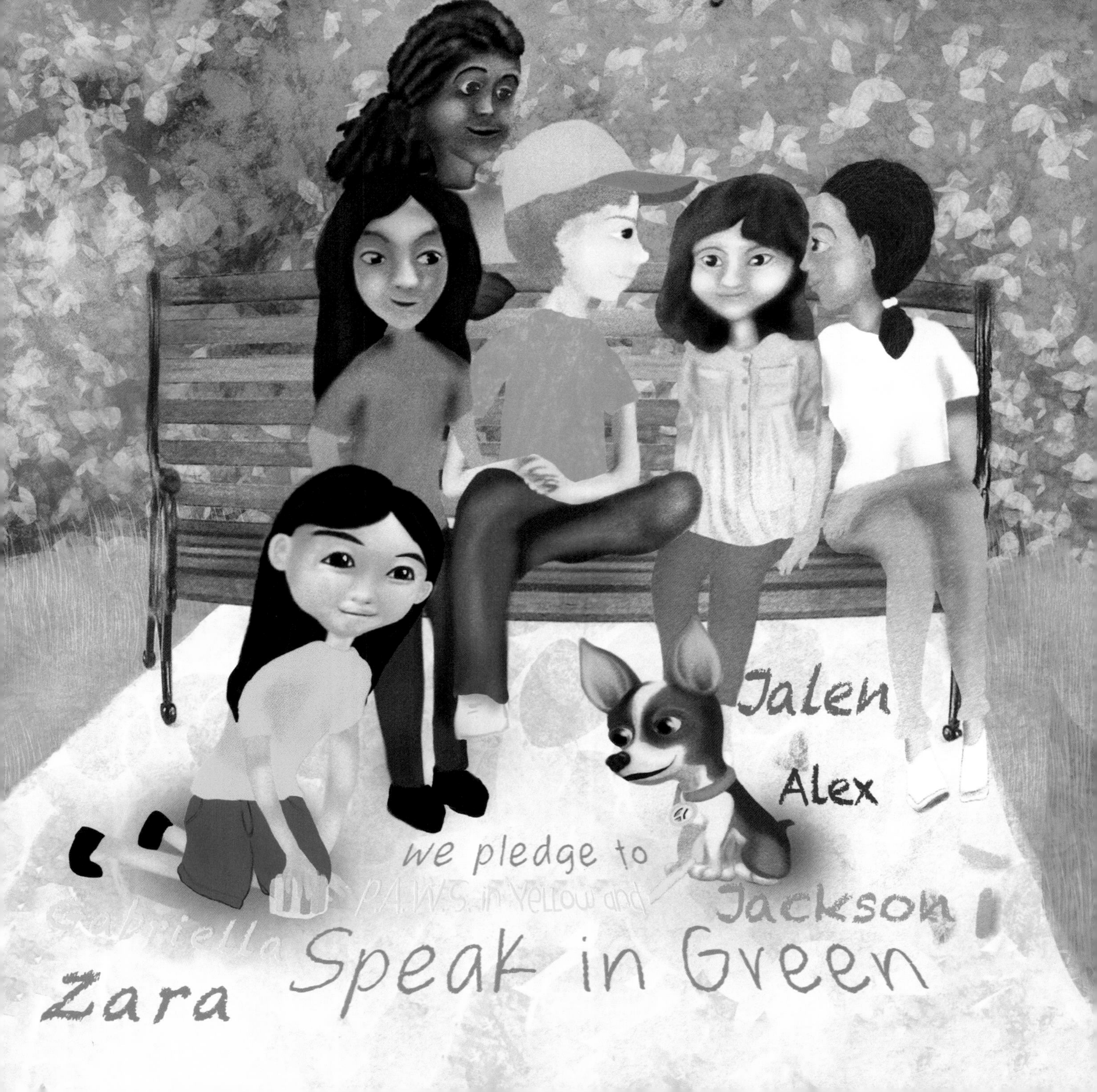

we pledge to
P.A.W.S. in Yellow and
Gabriella

Zara

Speak in Green

Jalen

Alex

Jackson

"It's great that we talked instead of yelled. We can help our friends and family to P.A.W.S. in Yellow and Speak in Green like Miss Emma helped us," said Alex.

"Yes!" Jackson said. "We're a team! We know how to stop, take a deep breath, listen, and understand each other."
"Team Speaking in Green!"

"Hi, Petey Peace," said Gabriella cheerfully.

"Are you ready to walk home with us?"

"Yogee! Was the rest of your day peaceful?" asked Petey Peace.

"That's how Petey Peace says, 'yes'," Gabriella explained to her friends.

"Yogee!" they all laughed. "Now that we know how to be mediators, we will always feel peaceful. We know how to Speak in Green!"

SPEAKING IN GREEN
PICTURE DICTIONARY

PICTURE DICTIONARY

Muttered

To say something in a low voice, especially when upset.

"I will never play with you again if you don't say it," *muttered* Jackson.

Compassionate

Showing or feeling concerned for someone else and wanting to help them feel better.

"You're all sincere and compassionate children."

Interjected

To interrupt or throw in a comment when someone else is speaking.

"She refused to say she was sorry," Zara interjected.

Attentively

Paying attention to what someone else is saying.

"OK. Let's listen attentively to one another."

Inquired

To ask a question.

"What do you all think you could do?" Miss Emma inquired.

Mediation

To work with two people or groups who disagree with each other and help them come to a peaceful agreement.

"Does everyone agree to a peaceful mediation."

PICTURE DICTIONARY

Suggested

To mention or offer a possible way something may be said or done.

"Maybe we could all talk with each other," Alex suggested to the group.

Murmured

Speaking in a tone that is quiet and soft.

"Me too," murmured Jackson reluctantly.

Reluctantly

Unwilling or not eager to do or say something.

"Me too," murmured Jackson reluctantly.

Apologetically

Feeling sorry for something said or done.

"This won't happen with any other new student," Alex said apologetically.

Encouragingly

To inspire someone or causing a hopeful feeling.

"Jackson, please share your thoughts about what happened today," said Miss Emma encouragingly.

Taunted

To say something mean in order to upset or anger a person.
Differs from teasing which is playful and friendly.

"Some kids taunted me about my dreadlocks."

PICTURE DICTIONARY

Invisible

Something that cannot be seen.

A feeling of being unnoticed.

"Since I moved here from Mexico, I feel like I'm invisible."

Hijab

A scarf worn by Muslim women who choose to cover their hair and neck, and sometimes their face, hands, and feet.

"People say ugly things about my mother's hijab."

Extending

To stretch out and reach for something.

"Jackson smiled extending his hand to help her stand."

Frustrated

Very unhappy, angry or upset because of being unable to say, do, or feel something.

"I was frustrated and I took it out on Jackson."

Empathy

The ability to share and understand what someone else is feeling.

"Let's make a pledge to be caring, understanding, and show empathy for each other."

Mediators

People who help others work out their conflicts peacefully.

"Now that we know how to be mediators, we will always feel peaceful."

Please write the
Green Words from the
Rolling into Peace story

Green Words

_____

_____
_____
_____
_____
_____
_____
_____
_____
_____
_____

Green Words

_____

_____
_____
_____
_____
_____
_____
_____
_____
_____
_____

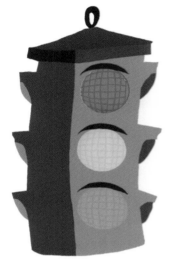 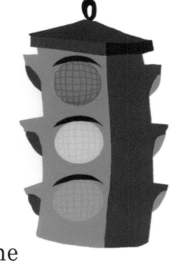

Please write the
Red Words from the
Rolling into Peace story

Red Words

_____

_____

_____

_____

_____

_____

_____

_____

_____

_____

_____

_____

Red Words

_____

_____

_____

_____

_____

_____

_____

_____

_____

_____

_____

_____

Petey Peace's

AWARD

for

Speaking in Green

Presented to

_____

_____   _____
Date   Signed

"Be a rainbow in someone's cloud."

-Maya Angelou

Pause to breathe

Acknowledge what is said

Welcome good thoughts

Shift to Green

Erica D. Babino is an author, mediator, and treatment advocate. Since receiving certificates in Basic Mediation Training, Divorce and Family, and Parenting Coordination starting in 2008, Erica realized that she wanted to help young children learn to manage conflict. *Rolling into Peace* and the other forthcoming books in the Speaking in Green series was inspired by the past and present political and social climate in our world. Passionate about the water, Erica relaxes by swimming, kayaking, and meditating. She is most grateful for family, friends, and scrumptious vegan food. Erica is currently looking for her very own, real life Petey Peace.

Illustrator, **Robinson Pyles** is also a computer technician, creative consultant, and author. Robinson enjoys camping, stargazing, Sudoku, and watching horror movies. This self-taught artist started as an illustrator for Speaking in Green's *Rolling into Peace.* Through his artistic expression, he has now become an integral part of the movement to help young children use Green Words to enhance their conflict resolution skills. Robinson is most grateful for his gift of creativity and quirky mind.

CPSIA information can be obtained at www.ICGtesting.com
Printed in the USA
BVIW12n2339081017
497098BV00002B/2